Midnight Magic

Mirror Mischief

For Jack. Another cat! Sorry.
— MH

For Noah, and his humans, Sam and Nick. xx
— EE

STRIPES PUBLISHING LIMITED
An imprint of the Little Tiger Group
1 Coda Studios, 189 Munster Road, London SW6 6AW

Imported into the EEA by Penguin Random House Ireland,
Morrison Chambers, 32 Nassau Street, Dublin D02 YH68

www.littletiger.co.uk

First published in Great Britain in 2021
Text copyright © Michelle Harrison, 2021
Illustrations © Elissa Elwick, 2021

ISBN: 978-1-78895-149-4

The right of Michelle Harrison and Elissa Elwick to be identified as
the author and illustrator of this work respectively has been asserted by them
in accordance with the Copyright, Designs and Patents Act, 1988.

Printed and bound in China.

MIX
Paper from
responsible sources
FSC® C020056

The Forest Stewardship Council® (FSC®) is a global, not-for-profit organization dedicated to
the promotion of responsible forest management worldwide. FSC defines standards based
on agreed principles for responsible forest stewardship that are supported by environmental,
social, and economic stakeholders. To learn more, visit www.fsc.org

STP/1800/0404/0521

2 4 6 8 10 9 7 5 3 1

Michelle Harrison ★ Elissa Elwick

Midnight Magic

Mirror Mischief

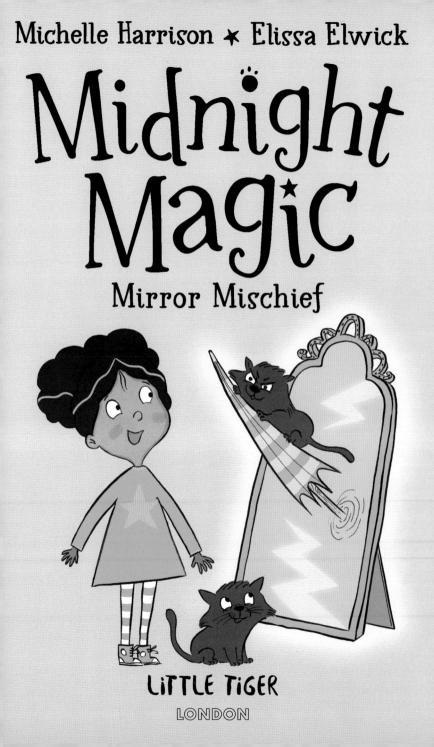

LITTLE TIGER

LONDON

Black cats born at midnight
Are different indeed,
A mischievous, odd
And peculiar breed.

For in every whisker
And each tuft of fur,
In every pounce
And every purr...

There's magic (yes, **MAGIC!**)
And strong stuff at that!
And Midnight is one
Of these rare types of cat...

Chapter
One

At breakfast one morning
A little girl sat
Whispering to her
Unusual cat.

"**Oh, Midnight,**" she said.
"Don't worry, I'll only
Be gone a few hours.
Please, don't feel too lonely."

Midnight looked up at
The clock on the wall.
Soon her best friend would
Be leaving for school.

Hours without Trixie —
How gloomy. How bleak!
And worse, she had school
Five whole days every week!

Midnight had wandered
The streets as a stray
Before Trixie begged
Dad to let the cat stay.

They all lived together
With Doodle the hound
And her cat-loving nan
The **purr-fect** home found.

Midnight's broom Twiggy
Moved in with them too.
At first Trixie's family
Hadn't a clue

That magic had entered
The household that day
But soon they found out
It was with them to stay!

"School in ten minutes!"
Dad said with a smile,
Ironing a shirt
From a teetering pile.

Aha! Midnight plotted.
Ten minutes? You think?
Oh, I can fix that with
A magical wink...

Smoke puffed from her whiskers
And curled round the clock.
Its **tocks** became **ticks**
And the **ticks** now went **tock**!

The clock's hands turned back
And Trix gave a grin
While tickling her cat's
Soft and fluffy black chin.

"There's heaps of time, look!"
She said. "We've got plenty!"
Ten minutes ... fifteen!
Soon it was twenty.

They knew it was naughty,
The mischievous pair.
They knew Dad might catch them
But they didn't care!

"Bravo!" Trixie whispered.
"You're so very clever.
Now we've got more time
To have **fun** together!"

So Midnight created
A cereal mountain
Inside Trixie's bowl
With a chocolate-milk fountain.

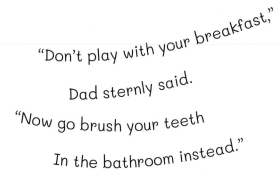

"Don't play with your breakfast,"

Dad sternly said.

"Now go brush your teeth

In the bathroom instead."

Even though Midnight
Had made a delay
She still knew that Trix
Would soon leave for the day.

Who can I play with?
What can I do?
Dad would be working.
And Nan was out too.

Doodle **loved** games
But he could be a pest,
For chasing poor Twiggy
Was what he liked best!

Trix got her toothbrush.
She started to scrub
While Midnight looked on
From the side of the tub.

And then Midnight had
A fantastic idea.
A way she could have fun
Without Trixie here.

A big oval mirror
Hung high on a hook.
All it would take
Was one little look...

Midnight jumped nearer,
Up on to the sink
Then gave her reflection
A magical wink.

Well, as you'd expect
The reflection *winked* too.
But out of its whiskers
Smoke billowed and blew!

Trix stared at the mirror,
Becoming aware
That something **amazing**
Was happening there.

For while her own Midnight
Was sitting beside her,
The **mirror cat** walked up
The wall like a spider.

It leaped on the shelf
And one swipe of its paw

Sent Dad's favourite
Aftershave **CRASH** to the floor!

And then it jumped down
To make Trixie laugh
By skating on soap
Round the edge of the bath.

It *winked* at the taps
On the bath and the sink
Before sticking out
Its long tongue for a drink.

Trixie and Midnight
Shared glances of glee.
Their side of the mirror
Was quite dry, you see!

For all of this havoc
Was just a reflection.
They couldn't be blamed —
It was mischief perfection!

Wink! Mirror Trix had
A shaving-foam beard.
Then written in toothpaste
A message appeared.

Smeared on the looking glass,
Gloopy and thick,
Trix read it aloud:
"Now let me out quick!"

Uh-uh! Midnight knew
That would be a mistake.
TWO magic cats would
Be too much to take!

now let me out quick

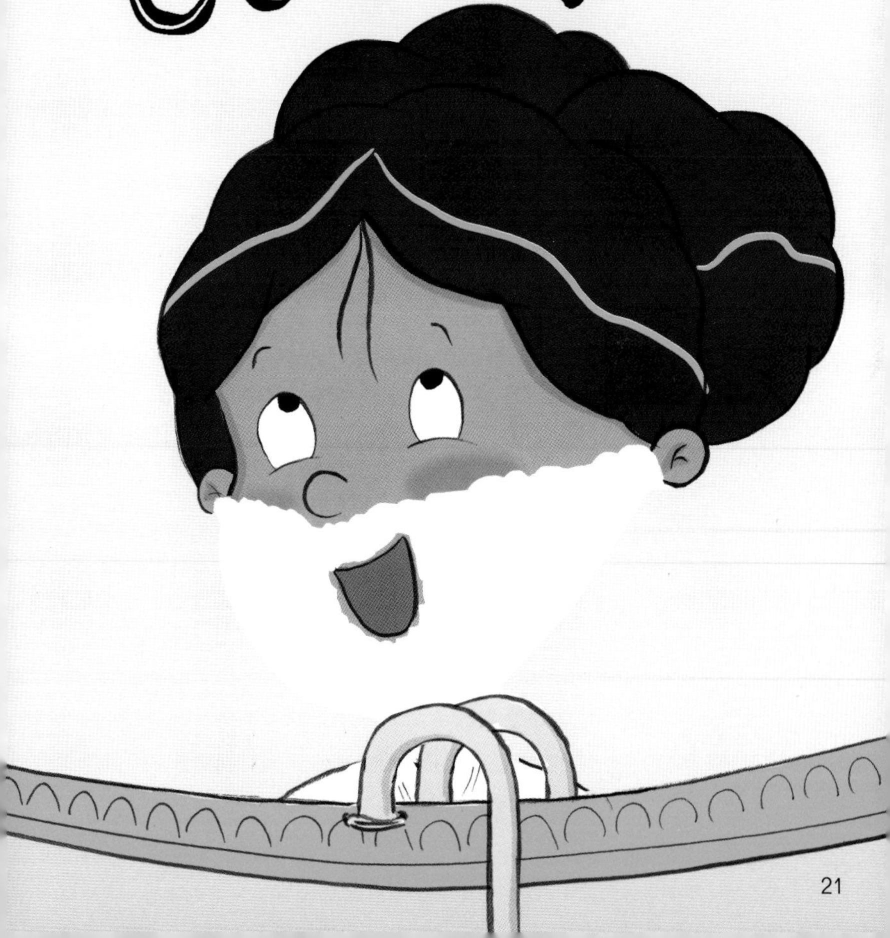

Down in the kitchen
Dad let out a shout:
"The clock's ticking backwards!"
Oh, rats — he'd found out!

"Midnight," Dad grumbled.
"Did *you* make us late?
We should have left home
At a quarter past eight!

"Remember!" he boomed.
"Your number one rule
Is *not* to do magic
While Trixie's at school!

"Homework! P.E. kit!
School jumper on!
WHERE are the car keys?"
And then they were gone.

But now Midnight didn't
Feel nearly so glum.

How could she be bored
With a new mirror chum?

Chapter Two

The fanciest mirror
Was by the front door
Where Twiggy was sweeping
Up leaves on the floor.

There Midnight's reflection
Winked at the coats
And boots and umbrellas
To make them all float.

In trotted Doodle,
Who fancied a snooze.
His basket was there
In the hall by the shoes.

Uh-oh! He spied Twiggy,
Who suddenly froze
For Doodle had quickly
Forgotten his doze.

Over the floorboards
Came *clattering claws*
And hot, whiffy breath
From *slobbering jaws*...

Doodle was really
Quite mad about Twig.
A stick to play fetch with!
This stick was **SO BIG!**

Twiggy took off
In a bit of a flap
And narrowly missed
The dog's teeth going **SNAP!**

But Twiggy was clumsy,
The hallway was small...
The broom hit the looking glass
Up on the wall.

It fell off the hook!
The mirror was **shattered**!
Fragments of glass were
Haphazardly scattered.

Oh dear, thought Midnight.
She stood in a huddle
With Twiggy and Doodle.
They **WERE** in muddle!

Alas, this was only
The start of the trouble
For out of the shards sprang
The mischievous double!

Exactly like Midnight
From whiskers to paws
With oodles of magic
And **razor-sharp claws**.

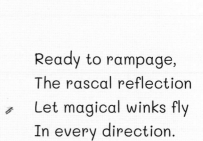

Ready to rampage,
The rascal reflection
Let magical winks fly
In every direction.

The coats came alive,
So did the wellies.
Poor Doodle, he shivered
And shook like a jelly.

Shoes going walkies
Without feet inside?
Help! Doodle thought
And rushed off to hide.

The **copycat** ran,
Leaping over the boots
So Midnight and Twiggy
Joined in the pursuit.

Midnight was quick
But her double was faster.
Each time she caught up
It somehow *slipped* past her.

It knotted Nan's knitting,

And rode Trixie's scooter.

It scratched all the chairs and

Blew up the computer!

How could they catch it —
This bundle of tricks?
Perhaps this was something
That magic could fix?

Midnight *winked* fast
But her powers alone
Were clearly no match
For the terrible clone.

All morning they chased it,
The time ticked away.
Trixie would soon finish
School for the day.

Plant pots were broken,
Flowers beheaded,
Cushions ripped open
Newspapers shredded.

The bathroom was next
On the copycat's list,
It *winked* at the taps
And the air filled with mist.

The loo roll unraveled
And slid like a snake.
How Midnight wished
To undo her mistake!

And then came the sound
Of a key in a lock.
Trixie and Dad were
Both in for a shock.

The front door swung open.
Dad gave a loud squeak.
"The mirror," he cried.
"It was an *antique*!"

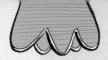

They stared at the shoes
They'd left neatly in pairs
Now in a race to
The top of the stairs.

They ducked under coats
That were flying above
And Trixie shook hands
With an old woolly glove.

41

Dad stormed up the stairs
And Twig followed after,
With Trixie behind them
Shaking with laughter.

Something *whipped* past them —
A ball of black fur!
And then came *another*
Both gone in a blur...

"EUREKA!" said Trixie
As Dad stood and gaped.
"Midnight's reflection —
It must have **escaped**!"

Could **TWO** cats, she wondered,
Be better than one?
Double the magic,
And double the **FUN**?

But then from the bathroom,
Full up with vapour,
A **thing** captured Dad —
A loop of loo paper!

Dad shook his ankle,
He couldn't get free!
Soon it had bound him
Right up to the knee!

And seeing her dad
All nervous and wriggly
Made Trixie feel cross and
Not nearly so giggly.

Chapter
Three

"**T**rixie!" yelled Dad.
"Escape while you can!"
So she backed away ...
And bumped into Nan.

"What's going on here?"
Nan asked in alarm,
Holding her yoga mat
Under her arm.

"Midnight's reflection,"
Gasped Trixie. **"It's out!**
It broke through the mirror.
It's chasing about!

"**Look!** In your room, Nan!
Midnight's there too.
Perhaps we can help her,
She'll know what to do."

"What if she **doesn't**?"
Nan looked uncertain,
Watching the mirror cat
Climb up the curtain.

"Get back in your mirror!"
Nan scolded. "Now, shoo!"
The cat, looking smug,
Gave an insolent mew.

Eyes full of mischief,
Enjoying itself,
The copycat *winked*
At Nan's things on the shelf.

A wisp of smoke wrapped
Round Nan's teeth in a glass.
(She hadn't worn them
To hot yoga class.)

They **snapped** into life
With a **nip** and a **gnash**,
Eating their way through
The glass in a flash!

They munched up the rug
With a bloody-thirsty **ROAR**,
Chewing a hole
All the way through Nan's door.

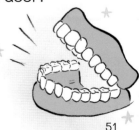

Crumbs! Midnight thought.
We're in for it now!
Her double agreed
With a wicked *Meow!*

It leaped on the light shade,
And did a neat *swoop,*
Then swung like a chimp,
With its tail in a loop.

"Midnight," asked Trixie,
"Could that cat be taught
Better behaviour
If it's ever caught?"

It didn't seem likely
But heck, she could try!
Here goes, Midnight thought as
She pounced way up high.

Oh, no! Even though
Midnight's aim had been great
She reached her reflection
A whisker too late!

Doink went the light shade
Straight over her head.
Meanwhile, the double
Bounced on to the bed.

Duck feather pillows,
Now these **WERE** a treat!
And wallpaper covered
In bluebirds — how sweet!

A cheeky wink here
Sent smoke flying there
And suddenly birds filled
The room everywhere!

Nan's pillows were quacking!
The air rang with tweets!
The double chased birds
As they swooped past the sheets!

Midnight escaped from
The shade round her neck,
Just *ducking* a beak
And *dodging* a peck.

Those birdies looked **TASTY!**
Dare she join in
And be just as **BAD**
As her terrible twin?

Hmm, Midnight pondered,
Mouth starting to water,
*It's hard to resist but
I don't think I oughta!*

She **couldn't** let Trix down,
Her very best friend!
And so Midnight chose
To behave in the end.

Meow! Midnight said,
And she sprang into action,
Refusing to let
The birds be a distraction.

The copycat legged it
At breathtaking pace!
Nan, Trix and Midnight
And Twiggy gave chase!

But out in the hall
Was a *horrible* sight —
A toilet roll monster,
Enormous and white.

The thing lurched straight at them,
A bumbling **beast**
With Nan's teeth behind it
In search of a **FEAST!**

"Quick! Run for your lives!
It's a mummy!" Nan cried.
None of them guessed
It was Dad stuck inside.

"After that copycat,
Don't let it hide!
Twig!" Trixie said,
"Will you give us a ride?"

Twig hovered low for
The gang to climb on.
"Hey, wait!" mumbled Dad
But too late, they were gone!

They *whooshed* down the stairs
With Nan at the rear
And Trix in the middle
So Midnight could steer.

Birds flying with them
Above and below,
They searched for the double.
Now where did it go?

Midnight's sharp ears caught
The sound of a **CLUNK**
From the old cupboard
Full up with their junk.

"Aha!" Trixie yelled
As she threw the door wide,
Revealing the copycat
Lurking inside.

Then Trixie spied it —
Her old fishing net!
By an inflatable
Beach jumbo jet.

She grabbed it and scooped...
Just a moment too late.
A copycat wink
Made the jet plane inflate!

Into the plane
The cat went with a hop
It took off and **FLEW**
Then suddenly...

POP!

The cat's claws had *burst* it!
Oh, what a din!
It **CRASHED** in the kitchen —
Dare they go in?

Chapter
Four

They peeked round the corner.

The mugs were all smashed!

The plates were in pieces,

The kitchen was **TRASHED!**

A snowdrift of sugar,
A chewed pack of ham,
Sticky red paw prints
In strawberry jam...

"**Yikes!**" Trixie whispered
As Nan gave a wail.
For there at the end of
The terrible trail

Midnight's reflection
Sat licking its toes
With sugary whiskers
And jam on its nose.

Swishing its tail like
A villainous cloak,
The cat disappeared
In a puff of green smoke!

"**DISASTER!**" cried Trixie.
"Where could it be?
How can we catch
A cat no one can *see*?"

MUNCH. They all heard it,
A curious sound.
It came from the cupboard.
The cat had been found!

There! Scoffing biscuits
Of Midnight's (and Doodle's)
Inside the wok that
Dad used to cook noodles.

Doodle squeezed out
From under a chair.
They were **HIS** biscuits
And *he* didn't share!

He rushed to attack,
Suddenly brave.
Dog to the rescue!
BISCUITS TO SAVE!

But swiftly the double
Took off. It was flying!
"Down!" Nan demanded.
"That wok is for **frying**!"

The pan left the kitchen
Then quick as a flea
It flew up the chimney —
The double was **FREE!**

Twiggy shot after it.
Gosh, what a *squeeze*.
Soot scattered everywhere,
Making them sneeze.

They got halfway up
And were covered in muck
Then couldn't go further —
Nan's bottom was stuck!

But Midnight was clever.
With one magic wink
She tackled the problem
By making them shrink!

Tiny as beetles,
Unstuck at last,
They shot out the chimney
In one sooty **BLAST**.

Trixie gasped, "That's *much*
More fun than the door!
Bet no one's swept
Chimneys like *that* before!"

Nan lost her balance
And fell with a *plop*.
She called from the roof,
"Keep going! Don't stop!"

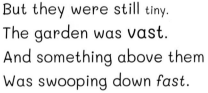

But they were still tiny.
The garden was **vast**.
And something above them
Was swooping down *fast*.

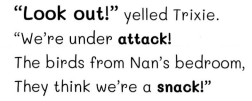

"Look out!" yelled Trixie.
"We're under **attack!**
The birds from Nan's bedroom,
They think we're a **snack!**"

"There," Trixie pointed.
"Next to the slide.
The watering can
Is a good place to hide!"

They darted inside it
(And easily fitted).
PHEW! They were safe.
Those birds were outwitted!

Trix spied the copycat,
Tail madly *swishing*,
Dipping its paw in the pond.
It was **fishing**!

"Hurry!" she cried,
Twig took off at speed...
This time they'd catch it!
They *had* to succeed.

The grass was a jungle
With worms large as snakes!
And frogs big as dogs
In the pond — now a lake.

"Midnight," gasped Trix,
Gazing down from the air.
"The pond! Our reflection...
Your one isn't there!"

Trixie had spotted
An obvious clue
And suddenly Midnight
Knew *just* what to do!

With Midnight's gang sooty
And still very small,
The double could not see
Them coming at all...

A wink took them back
To their usual size
And then Midnight charged
With a mew of, **"Surprise!"**

She caught her reflection.
They both *tumbled* in,
Spitting out pondweed,
Soaked to the skin!

YUCK! It was horrid
And freezing and **WET**!
The worstest thing ever —
Much worse than the **VET**!

But when she got out
(Now clean and soot-free)
Midnight's reflection
Stayed where it **SHOULD** be!

A cross little face
In the water. **Hooray!**
Trix picked up the wok and
They went on their way.

Indoors to blankets!
And hot baths! And hugs!
And flasks of hot chocolate
(Cos there were no mugs).

Dad was no longer
A toilet roll yeti.
Nan's false teeth were lifeless
In piles of confetti.

Once they were dry
Midnight started to **fix**
All of the mirror cat's
Trouble and **tricks**.

At last it was tidy,
Their broken things mended.
Thankfully copycat
Chaos had ended!

"Midnight," said Trix as
They curled up together.
**"We're a great team.
We'll be best friends forever."**

Snug on the sofa
They cuddled up tight.
The **mischief** was over...
At least for **tonight!**

A Note from Midnight:

Did you know that black cats like me are often the last to be picked from animal shelters? Sadly, it's true! People tend to choose cats with more unusual colours or markings. Sometimes black cats wait months — or even years — before finding a home.

So if you're thinking of getting a cat, keep in mind that black ones have just as much love to give. Some people even think we are lucky!

Remember to check out your local animal rescue centres, and give older cats a chance too. They can be just as playful as kittens!